MILLY-
MOLLY-
MANDY'S
SCHOOLDAYS

Publisher's Note
The stories in this collection are reproduced in the form in which they appeared
upon first publication in the UK by George G. Harrap & Co. Ltd.
All spellings remain consistent with these original editions

KINGFISHER
An imprint of Kingfisher Publications Plc
New Penderel House, 283–288 High Holborn
London WC1V 7HZ
www.kingfisherpub.com

First published by Kingfisher 2005
2 4 6 8 10 9 7 5 3

The stories in this collection first appeared in
Milly-Molly-Mandy Stories (1928)
Milly-Molly-Mandy Again (1948)
Milly-Molly-Mandy and Billy Blunt (1967)
published by George G. Harrap & Co. Ltd.

Text and illustrations copyright © Joyce Lankester Brisley,
1928, 1948, 1967
Cover illustrations copyright © Clara Vulliamy 2000

A CIP catalogue record for this book is available from the British Library.

ISBN 0 7534 1126 1
Printed in India
2TR/0405/THOM/HBM(PICA)/115GSM/F

MILLY-
MOLLY-
MANDY'S

SCHOOLDAYS

JOYCE LANKESTER BRISLEY

KINGFISHER

CONTENTS

MILLY-MOLLY-MANDY
GETS TO KNOW TEACHER

ONCE UPON A TIME there were changes at Milly-Molly-Mandy's school. Miss Sheppard, the head-mistress, was going away, and Miss Edwards, the second teacher, was to be head-mistress in her place, and live in the teacher's cottage just by the school, instead of coming in by the bus from the town each day.

Miss Edwards was very strict, and taught arithmetic and history and geography, and wore high collars.

Milly-Molly-Mandy wasn't particularly interested in the change, though she liked both Miss Sheppard and Miss Edwards quite well. But one afternoon Miss Edwards gave her a note to give to her Mother, and the note was to ask if Milly-Molly-Mandy's Mother would be so very good as to let Miss Edwards have a bed at the nice white cottage with the thatched roof for a night or two until Miss Edwards got her new little house straight.

Father and Mother and Grandpa and Grandma and Uncle and Aunty talked it over during supper, and they thought they might manage it for a few nights.

Milly-Molly-Mandy was very interested, and tried to think what it would be like to have Teacher sitting at supper with them, and going to sleep in the spare room, as well as teaching in school all day. And she couldn't help feeling just a little bit glad that it was only to be for a night or two.

Next day she took a note to school for Teacher from Mother, to say, yes, they would be pleased to have her. And after school Milly-Molly-Mandy told little-friend-Susan and Billy Blunt about it.

And little-friend-Susan said, "Ooh! Won't you have to behave properly! I'm glad she's not coming to us!"

And Billy Blunt said, "Huh! – hard lines!"

Milly-Molly-Mandy was quite glad Teacher was only coming to stay for a few nights.

Miss Edwards arrived at the nice white cottage with the thatched roof just before supper time the following evening.

Milly-Molly-Mandy was looking out for her, and directly she heard the gate click she called Mother and ran and opened the front door wide, so that the hall lamp could shine down the path. And Teacher came in out of the dark, just as Mother hurried from the kitchen to welcome her.

Teacher thanked Mother very much for having her, and said she felt so dusty and untidy because she had been putting up shelves in her new little cottage ever since school was over.

So Mother said, "Come right up to your room, Miss Edwards, and Milly-Molly-Mandy will bring you a jug of hot water. And then I expect you'll be glad of some supper straight away!"

So Milly-Molly-Mandy ran along to the kitchen for a jug of hot water, thinking how funny it was to hear Teacher's familiar voice away from school. She tapped very politely at the half-open door of the spare room (she could see Teacher tidying her hair in front of the dressing-table, by the candlelight), and Teacher smiled at her as she took the steaming jug, and said:

"That's kind of you, Milly-Molly-Mandy! This is just what I want most. What a lovely smell of hot cakes!"

Milly-Molly-Mandy smiled back, though she was quite a bit surprised that Teacher should speak in that pleased, hungry sort of way – it was more the kind of way she, or little-friend-Susan, or Father or Mother or Grandpa or Grandma or Uncle or Aunty, might have spoken.

When Teacher came downstairs to the kitchen they all sat down to supper. Teacher's place was just opposite Milly-Molly-Mandy's and every time she caught Milly-Molly-Mandy's eye she smiled across at her. And Milly-Molly-Mandy smiled back, and tried to remember to sit up, for she kept on almost expecting Teacher to say, "Head up, Milly-Molly-Mandy! Keep your elbows off the desk!" – but she never did!

They were all a little shy of Teacher, just at first; but soon Father and Mother and Grandpa and Grandma and Uncle and Aunty were talking away, and Teacher was talking too, and laughing. And she looked so different when she was laughing that Milly-Molly-Mandy found it quite difficult to get on with her bread-and-milk before it got cold. Teacher enjoyed the hot cakes, and wanted to know just how Mother made them. She asked a lot of questions, and Mother said she would teach Teacher how to do it, so that she could make them in her own new little kitchen.

Milly-Molly-Mandy thought how funny it would be for Teacher to start having lessons.

After supper Teacher asked Milly-Molly-Mandy if she could make little sailor-girls, and when Milly-Molly-Mandy said no, Teacher drew a little sailor-girl, with a sailor-collar and sailor-hat and pleated skirt, on a folded piece of paper, and then she cut it out with Aunty's scissors. And when she unfolded the paper there was a whole row of little sailor-girls all holding hands.

Milly-Molly-Mandy did like it. She thought

how funny it was that she should have known Teacher all that time and never known she could draw little sailor-girls.

Then Mother said, "Now, Milly-Molly-Mandy, it is bedtime." So Milly-Molly-Mandy kissed Father and Mother and Grandpa and Grandma and Uncle and Aunty, and went to shake hands with Teacher. But Teacher said she wanted a kiss too. So they kissed each other in quite a nice friendly way.

But still Milly-Molly-Mandy felt when she went upstairs she must get into bed extra quickly and quietly, because Teacher was in the house.

Next morning Milly-Molly-Mandy and Teacher went to school together. And as soon as they got there Teacher was just her usual self again, and told Milly-Molly-Mandy to sit up, or to get on with her work, as if she had never laughed at supper, or cut out little sailor-girls, or kissed anyone goodnight.

After school Milly-Molly-Mandy showed little-friend-Susan and Billy Blunt the row of little sailor-girls.

And little-friend-Susan opened her eyes and

said, "Just fancy Teacher doing that!"

And Billy Blunt folded them up carefully in the creases so that he could see how they were made, and then he grinned and gave them back.

And little-friend-Susan and Billy Blunt didn't feel so very sorry for Milly-Molly-Mandy having Teacher to stay, then.

That evening Teacher came up to the nice white cottage with the thatched roof earlier than she did the day before. And when Milly-Molly-Mandy came into the kitchen from taking a nice meal out to Toby the dog, and giving him a good bedtime romp round the yard, what did she see but Teacher, with one of Mother's big aprons on and her sleeves tucked up, learning how to make apple turn-overs for supper! And Mother was saying, "Always mix pastry with a light hand," and Teacher was looking so interested, and didn't seem in the least to know she had a streak of flour down one cheek.

When Teacher saw Milly-Molly-Mandy she said, "Come along, Milly-Molly-Mandy, and have a cooking lesson with me, it's such fun!"

11

What did she see but Teacher learning how to make apple turn-overs

So Milly-Molly-Mandy's Mother gave her a little piece of dough, and she stood by Teacher's side, rolling it out and making it into a ball again; but she was much more interested in watching Teacher being taught. And Teacher did everything she was told, and tried so hard that her cheeks got quite pink.

When the turn-overs were all made there was a small piece of dough left on the board, so Teacher shaped it into the most beautiful little bird; and the bird and the turn-overs were all popped into the oven, together with Milly-Molly-Mandy's piece (which had been a pig and a cat and a teapot, but ended up a little grey loaf).

When Father and Mother and Grandpa and Grandma and Uncle and Aunty and Teacher and Milly-Molly-Mandy sat down to supper, Teacher put her finger on her lips to Milly-Molly-Mandy when the apple turn-overs came on, so that Milly-Molly-Mandy shouldn't tell who made them until they had been tasted. And Teacher watched anxiously, and presently Mother said, "How do you like these turn-overs?" And everybody said they were most delicious, and then Milly-Molly-Mandy couldn't wait any longer, and she called out, "Teacher made them!" and everybody was so surprised.

Milly-Molly-Mandy didn't eat the little grey-brown loaf, because she didn't quite fancy it (Toby the dog did, though), and she felt she couldn't eat the little golden-brown bird, because it really looked too good to be eaten just yet. So she took it to school with her next day, to share with little-friend-Susan and Billy Blunt.

And little-friend-Susan said, "Isn't it pretty? Isn't Teacher clever?"

And Billy Blunt said, "Fancy Teacher playing with dough!"

And little-friend-Susan and Billy Blunt didn't feel at all sorry for Milly-Molly-Mandy having Teacher to stay, then.

The next day was Saturday, and Teacher's furniture had come, and she was busy all day arranging it and getting the curtains and the pictures up. And Milly-Molly-Mandy with little-friend-Susan and Billy Blunt came in the afternoon to help. And they ran up and down

stairs, and fetched hammers and nails, and
held things, and made themselves very useful
indeed.

And at four o'clock Teacher sent Billy Blunt
out to get some cakes from Mrs Hubble's shop,
while the others laid the table in the pretty
little sitting-room. And they had a nice kind of
picnic, with Milly-Molly-Mandy and little-
friend-Susan sharing a cup, and Billy Blunt
having a saucer for a plate, because everything
wasn't unpacked yet. And they all laughed and
talked, and were as happy as anything. And
when Teacher said it was time to send them all
off home Milly-Molly-Mandy was so sorry to

think Teacher wasn't coming to sleep in the spare room any more that she wanted to kiss Teacher without being asked. And she actually did it, too. And little-friend-Susan and Billy Blunt didn't look a bit surprised, either. And after that, somehow, it didn't seem to matter that Teacher was strict in school, for they knew that she was really just a very nice, usual sort of person inside all the time!

MILLY-MOLLY-MANDY
AND DUM-DUM

ONCE UPON A TIME Milly-Molly-Mandy was wandering past the Big House down by the crossroads where the little girl Jessamine, and her mother, Mrs Green, lived (only they were away just now).

There was always a lot of flowers in the garden of the Big House, so it was nice to peep through the gate when you passed. Besides, Mr Moggs, little-friend-Susan's father, worked there (he was the gardener), and Milly-Molly-Mandy could see him now, weeding with a long-handled hoe.

"Hello, Mr Moggs," Milly-Molly-Mandy called through the gate (softly, because you don't like to shout in other people's gardens, even when you know the people are away). "Could I come in, do you think?"

Mr Moggs looked up and said, "Well, now, I shouldn't wonder but that you could!"

So Milly-Molly-Mandy pushed open the big iron gate and slipped through.

"Isn't it pretty here!" she said, looking about her. "What do you weed it for, when there's nobody to see?"

"Ah," said Mr Moggs, "you learn it doesn't do to let things go, in a garden, or anywhere else. Weeds and all such like, they get to thinking they own the place if you let 'em alone awhile."

He went on scratching out weeds, so Milly-Molly-Mandy gathered them into his big wheelbarrow for him.

Presently Mr Moggs scratched out a worm along with a tuft of dandelion, and Milly-Molly-Mandy squeaked because she nearly took hold of it without noticing (only she just didn't).

"Don't you like worms?" asked Mr Moggs.

"No," said Milly-Molly-Mandy, "I don't!"

"Ah," said Mr Moggs. "I know someone who does, though."

"Who?" asked Milly-Molly-Mandy, sitting back on her heels.

"Old Dum-dum's very partial to a nice fat worm," said Mr Moggs. "Haven't you met old Dum-dum?"

"No," said Milly-Molly-Mandy. "Who's old Dum-dum?"

"You come and see," said Mr Moggs. "I've got to feed him before I go off home."

He trundled the barrow to the back garden and emptied it on the rubbish heap, and Milly-Molly-Mandy followed, carrying the worm on a trowel.

Mr Moggs got a little tin full of grain from the tool-shed, and pulled a lettuce from the vegetable bed, and then he went to the end of the garden, Milly-Molly-Mandy following.

There was a little square of grass fenced off with wire netting in which was a little wooden gate. And in the middle of the square of grass was a little round pond. And standing at the edge of the little round pond, looking very solemn, hunched up in his feathers, was Dum-dum.

"Oh!" said Milly-Molly-Mandy. "Dum-dum is a duck!"

"Well, he's a drake, really," said Mr Moggs. "See the little curly feathers on his tail? That shows he's a gentleman. Lady ducks don't have curls on their tails." He leaned over the netting and emptied the grain into a feeding-pan lying on the grass. "Come on, quack-quack!" said Mr Moggs. "Here's your supper."

Dum-dum looked round at him, and at Milly-Molly-Mandy. Then he waddled slowly over on his yellow webbed feet, and shuffled his beak in the pan for a moment. Then he waddled slowly back to his pond, dipped down and took a sip, and stood as before, looking very solemn, hunched up in his feathers, with a drop of water hanging from his flat yellow beak.

"He doesn't want any supper!" said Milly-Molly-Mandy. "Why doesn't he?"

"Feels lonely, that's what. Misses the folk up at the Big House. They used to come and talk to him sometimes and give him bits. He's the little girl Jessamine's pet."

"Poor Dum-dum!" said Milly-Molly-Mandy. "He does look miserable. Would you like a worm, Dum-dum?"

He came waddling over again, and stretched up his beak. And down went the worm, *snip-snap*.

"Doesn't he make a funny husky noise? Has he lost his quack?" asked Milly-Molly-Mandy.

"No," said Mr Moggs, "gentlemen ducks never talk so loud as lady ducks."

"*Huh! Huh! Huh!*" quacked Dum-dum, asking for more worms as loudly as he could.

So Milly-Molly-Mandy dug with the trowel and found another, a little one, and threw it over the netting.

"Do you suppose worms mind very much?" she asked, watching Dum-dum gobbling.

"Well, I don't suppose they think a great deal about it, one way or t'other," said Mr Moggs.

He dug over a bit of ground with his spade, and Milly-Molly-Mandy found eight more worms. So Dum-dum had quite a good supper after all.

Then Milly-Molly-Mandy leaned over the wire-netting and tried stroking the shiny green feathers on Dum-dum's head and neck. And though he edged away a bit at first, after a few tries he stood quite still, holding his head down while she stroked as if he rather liked it.

And then suddenly he turned and pushed his beak into Milly-Molly-Mandy's warm hand and left it there, so that she was holding his beak as if she were shaking hands with it! It startled her at first, it felt so funny and cold.

"Ah, he likes you," said Mr Moggs, wiping his spade with a bunch of grass. "He's a funny old bird; some he likes and some he doesn't. Well, we must be going."

"Mr Moggs," begged Milly-Molly-Mandy, still holding Dum-dum's beak gently in her hand, "don't you think I might come in sometimes to cheer him up, while his people are away? He's so lonely!"

"Well," said Mr Moggs, "I don't see why not – if you don't go bringing your little playmates running around in here too. Look, if I'm not about you can get in by the side gate there." And he showed her how to unfasten it and lock it up again. "But mind, I'm trusting you," said Mr Moggs.

So Milly-Molly-Mandy promised to be very careful indeed.

After that she went into the Big House garden every day after school, to cheer up poor Dum-dum. And he got so cheerful he would run to his fence to meet her, saying "*Huh! Huh! Huh!*" directly he heard her coming. She used to go into his enclosure to play with him, and pour water on to the earth for him to make mud with. (He loved mud!)

One day Milly-Molly-Mandy thought it would be nice if Dum-dum could have a change from that narrow run, so she asked Mr Moggs if she might let him out for a little walk. And Mr Moggs said she might try it, if she watched that he didn't eat the flowers and vegetables or get out into the road. So Milly-Molly-Mandy opened his little wooden gate, and Dum-dum stepped out on his yellow feet, looking at everything with great interest.

He was so good and obedient, he followed her along the garden paths and came where she called, like a little dog. So she often let him out after that. She turned over stones and things for him to hunt slugs and woodlice underneath. Sometimes she took him in the front garden too, and showed him to Billy Blunt through the gate.

One morning Milly-Molly-Mandy was very early for school, because the clock at home was fast. At first, when she found no-one round the school gate, she thought it was late; but when she found it wasn't she knew why little-friend-Susan hadn't been ready when she passed the Moggs's cottage!

So, as there was plenty of time, she thought she'd go and visit Dum-dum before school today. So she slipped in by the side gate, and found him busily tidying his feathers in the morning sunshine. He looked surprised and very pleased to see her, and they had a run round the garden and found one slug and five woodlice (which Dum-dum thought very tasty for breakfast!). Then she shut him back in his enclosure, and latched his little gate, and shut the side gate and fastened it as Mr Moggs had shown her, and went off to school. (And she only just wasn't late, this time!)

Well, they'd sung the hymn, and Miss Edwards had called their names, and everybody was there except Billy Blunt and the new little girl called Bunchy. And they had just settled down for an arithmetic lesson when the little girl Bunchy hurried in, looking rather frightened. And she told Miss Edwards there was a great big goose outside, and she dared not come in before because she thought it might bite her!

"A goose!" said Miss Edwards. "Nonsense! There are no geese round here."

And Milly-Molly-Mandy looked up from her exercise book quickly. But she knew she had shut Dum-dum up carefully, so she went on again dividing by seven (which wasn't easy).

And then the door opened again, and Billy Blunt came in with a wide grin on his face and a note in his hand. (It was from his mother to ask Miss Edwards to excuse his being late, because he'd had to run an errand for his father, who had no-one else to send.)

And who *do* you think came in with him, pushing between Billy Blunt's legs through the doorway, right into the schoolroom?

It was Dum-dum!

"Billy Blunt!" said Miss Edwards. "What is this?"

"I couldn't help it, ma'am," said Billy Blunt. "He would come in. I tried to shoo him off." (But I don't really think he had tried awfully hard!)

"You mustn't let it come in here," said Miss Edwards. "Turn it out. Sit down, children, and be quiet." (Because they were all out of their places, watching and laughing at the duck that came to school.)

"Oh, please, Teacher," said Milly-Molly-Mandy, putting up her hand.

Who DO you think came in with him?

"Sit down, Milly-Molly-Mandy," said Miss Edwards. "Take that duck outside, Billy Blunt. Quickly, now."

But when Billy Blunt tried again to shoo him out Dum-dum slipped away from him, farther in, under the nearest desk. And Miss Muggins's Jilly squealed loudly, and pulled her legs up on to her seat.

"Please, Teacher –" said Milly-Molly-Mandy again. "Oh, please, Teacher – he's my duck. I mean, he's a friend of mine."

"What is all this?" said Miss Edwards. "Be quiet, all of you! Now, Milly-Molly-Mandy – explain."

So Milly-Molly-Mandy explained who Dum-dum was, and where he lived, and that she thought he had come to look for her – though how he had got out and found his way here she couldn't think. "Please, Teacher, can I take him back home?" she asked.

"I can't let you go in the middle of school," said Miss Edwards. "You can shut him out in the yard now, and take him back after school."

So Milly-Molly-Mandy walked to the door, saying, "Come, Dum-dum!"

And Dum-dum ran waddling on his flapping yellow feet after her, all across the floor, saying "*Huh! Huh! Huh!*" as he went.

How the children did laugh!

Billy Blunt said, "I'll just see that the gate's shut." And he hurried outside too (lest Miss Edwards should say he needn't!)

He tried to stroke Dum-dum as Milly-Molly-Mandy did, but Dum-dum didn't know Billy Blunt well enough. He opened his beak wide and said "*Huhhh!*" at him. So Billy Blunt left off trying and went and shut the gate.

"He must have some water," said Milly-Molly-Mandy (because she knew ducks are never happy if they haven't).

So they looked about for something to hold
water, other than the drinking-mug. And Billy
Blunt brought the lid of the dustbox, and they
filled it at the drinking-tap and set it on the
ground. And Dum-dum at once began taking
sip after sip, as if he had never tasted such
nice water before.

So Milly-Molly-Mandy and Billy Blunt left
him there, and hurried back to their lessons.

Directly school was over the children
rushed out to see Milly-Molly-Mandy lead the
duck (drake, I mean) along the road back to
his home. (It wasn't easy with so many people
helping!) Mr Moggs was just coming away
from the Big House, but he went back with

her to find out how Dum-dum had escaped, for his gate was shut as Milly-Molly-Mandy had left it. And they found Dum-dum had made a little hole in his wire netting and pushed through that way and under the front gate. So Mr Moggs fastened up the hole.

And while he was doing it Milly-Molly-Mandy noticed that the windows were open in the Big House, and the curtains were drawn back.

"Oh!" said Milly-Molly-Mandy. "Have the people come back?"

"They're coming tomorrow," said Mr Moggs. "Mrs Moggs is just airing the place for them."

"Then I shan't be able to come and see Dum-dum any more!" said Milly-Molly-Mandy.

And she felt quite sad for some days after that, to think that Dum-dum wouldn't want her any more, though she was glad he wasn't lonely.

Then one day (what DO you think?) Milly-Molly-Mandy met the little girl Jessamine and her mother in the post-office, and the little girl Jessamine's mother said, "Mr Moggs tells me you used to come and cheer up our old duck while we were away!"

Milly-Molly-Mandy wondered if Mrs Green was cross about it. But she wasn't a bit. She said, "Jessamine is going to boarding school soon – did you know? – and she was wondering what to do about Dum-dum. Would you like to have him for keeps, when she has gone?"

And the little girl Jessamine said, "We want him to go to someone who'll be kind to him."

Milly-Molly-Mandy *was* pleased!

She ran home to give Father the stamps she had been sent to buy, and to ask the family if she might have Dum-dum for keeps.

And Mother said, "How kind of the Greens!"

And Father said, "He can live out in the meadow."

And Grandma said, "It will be very lonely for him."

And Grandpa said, "We must find him a companion."

And Aunty said, "You'll have to save up and buy another one."

And Uncle said, "I've been thinking of keeping a few ducks myself, down by the brook. Your Dum-dum can live along with them, if you like, Milly-Molly-Mandy."

Milly-Molly-Mandy was very pleased indeed.

The next day she hurried down to the Big House to tell the little girl Jessamine and her mother. And they let her take Dum-dum home with her at once.

So she led him slowly by the short cut across the fields to the nice white cottage with the thatched roof. And he followed her beautifully all the way. In fact, he walked right over the step and into the kitchen with her!

When Uncle saw him following her about he said:

"Milly-Molly had a duck.
    Its little head was green.
And everywhere that Milly went
    That duck was to be seen!"

"Yes, and he did follow me to school one day, like Mary's little lamb!" said Milly-Molly-Mandy.

And do you know, old Dum-dum didn't want to live down by the brook with the other ducks; it was too far from Milly-Molly-Mandy. He chose to live in the barn-yard with the cows and Twinkletoes the pony, and drink out of Toby the dog's drinking-bowl. And whenever the garden gate was undone Dum-dum would waddle straight through and make for the back door and knock on it with his beak, till Milly-Molly-Mandy came out to play with him!

MILLY-MOLLY-MANDY
AND A WET DAY

Once upon a time, one morning, when Milly-Molly-Mandy went off to school, it was raining and raining. (But she had on her rubber boots and raincoat and hood.)

When she got to the Moggs's cottage there was little-friend-Susan (in rubber boots and raincoat and hood) watching for her at the door.

"Oh, what a nasty wet, rainy day!" said little-friend-Susan, running out to join her.

"Mother says, if we keep going it won't hurt," said Milly-Molly-Mandy.

So they kept going, trudging along together down the wet road with the wet hedges each side, very glad to have each other to squeal to when the cold raindrops dripped off their noses.

When they got to the duck-pond all the little ducks were flapping and quacking away as if quite enjoying such a nice wet, rainy day! When they got to the village Billy Blunt (in thick shoes and raincoat) was dashing from the corn-shop; and Miss Muggins's niece Jilly (in new red rubber boots and her mackintosh over her head) was running from the draper's shop. They hadn't far to go, of course, but Milly-Molly-Mandy and little-friend-Susan arrived at school almost the same time, together with some other boys and girls who came by the red bus to the crossroads.

They all hung up their coats and hats and changed their shoes, flapping and quacking away together like a lot of little ducks, as if they too quite enjoyed the rainy day! (Milly-Molly-Mandy and little-friend-Susan were dry and warm as toast after their long walk.)

When morning school was over the rain had

stopped for a bit. But everywhere was still sopping wet, and in the road outside the school gate was a great muddy puddle.

Milly-Molly-Mandy, and a few others who went home for dinner (some who lived a long way off ate theirs at school), rather enjoyed having to wade through. Billy Blunt chose the deepest place. But Miss Muggins's Jilly, who tried to jump over, made a fine splash.

"It's a good thing we've got our mackintoshes on!" said Milly-Molly-Mandy.

"We ought to be ducks!" said little-friend-Susan.

"Road ought to be mended," said Billy Blunt.

He looked around and picked up some stones which he threw into the puddle. Milly-Molly-Mandy threw in a few bits of broken slate, and little-friend-Susan a handful of leaves and twigs. But it didn't make much difference.

"You'll get yourselves muddy," said Miss Muggins's Jilly.

"We need more stuff," said Billy Blunt.

So they looked about in hedges and ditches, picking up anything to throw in.

Miss Muggins's filly . . . tried to jump over

"Put 'em just here," said Billy Blunt. "No sense throwing them all over the place."

"I think I'd better go in now," said Miss Muggins's Jilly. "My aunty wouldn't like me to get my new rubber boots wet."

"I thought that's what rubber boots were for," said Milly-Molly-Mandy.

"They're wet already, anyhow," said little-friend-Susan.

"Don't stand there jabbering," said Billy Blunt. "Get busy, or get out of the way."

So Miss Muggins's Jilly went off home. But Milly-Molly-Mandy and little-friend-Susan and Billy Blunt carried on, looking for things to throw into the puddle.

They found some nice bits of brick on the waste ground by the crossroads. Also a splendid lump of broken paving-stone; but it was too heavy to carry, and they had to leave it after a struggle.

Then they had to hurry home to their dinners, and Milly-Molly-Mandy (with farthest to go) only *just* wasn't late for hers.

As soon as she could she hurried back to school, little-friend-Susan joining her on the way. But Billy Blunt was there already, adding fresh stones to mend the roadway. He had his box-on-wheels beside him.

"I got an idea while I was eating my pudding," said Billy Blunt. "We ought to be able to fetch that bit of paving-stone in this!"

So, with the little cart rattling and bumping along between them, they ran across the waste ground by the crossroads.

And together they heaved and they pushed and they grunted, till they got the stone out of the long grass, on to the little cart.

And then they pulled and they pushed, and they grunted, till they got it wheeled over the rough ground into the roadway.

And then they heaved and they grunted (which always seems to help!) till they slid the stone out into the middle of the puddle, with a fine muddy *splosh*!

"That's done it!" said Billy Blunt with satisfaction, wiping himself with some grass.

And then the bell rang, and they had to scurry in and tidy up.

When school was over everyone used the stepping-stones as they left, and kept dry and clean.

Then – what do you think? – as the bus that took some of the children home stopped for them at the crossroads a grey-haired lady got off, and came down to the school gate.

She asked Milly-Molly-Mandy, who was standing nearest:

"Has Miss Edwards come out yet? Would you mind telling her her mother's here?"

Milly-Molly-Mandy was surprised. (She had never thought of Teacher as having a mother!) Miss Edwards came hurrying out, very pleased, to welcome the visitor and take her into her own cottage next door. And they both used the stepping-stones and were glad

to find the road had been so nicely mended –
because Mrs Edwards hadn't any rubber
boots on, only lady's shoes and an umbrella.

"Well, now!" said Mother, when Milly-
Molly-Mandy came running home to the nice
white cottage with the thatched roof. "What
have you been up to? Have you got wet?"

"No!" said Milly-Molly-Mandy. "We kept
going, like you said, and I'm warm as anything!"

MILLY-MOLLY-MANDY
GOES EXCAVATING

ONCE UPON A TIME, as Milly-Molly-Mandy was going into school, she noticed a number of young men come striding along from the cross-roads and up Hooker's Hill. They were carrying spades and pickaxes and things, but somehow they didn't look like men who were mending the roads.

"I wonder what they're going to do," said Milly-Molly-Mandy.

"They're going to do excavating," said Billy Blunt. "I heard my dad talking about it. They've got permission."

"What's excavating?"

"Digging up old things," said Billy Blunt.

"Like buried treasure? That sort of thing? How do they know where to do it?"

"They guess," said Billy Blunt. "They guess Ancient Britons might have lived up there once. They just want to find out."

It sounded rather exciting. Milly-Molly-Mandy wished she could go digging instead of just going to school!

Next Saturday morning she took Toby the dog for a walk down to the village, rather hoping to hear more about the excavating. As she passed the corn-shop she saw Billy Blunt hanging over the side-gate.

"Hullo!" said Milly-Molly-Mandy. "What are you doing?"

Billy Blunt didn't answer. (Anyone could

see he was doing nothing.) But after a moment he said:

"Want to see something?"

Of course Milly-Molly-Mandy said yes, at once.

And Billy Blunt drew his hand slowly out of his pocket and opened it. There was a flat, round thing in it, streaked brown and green.

"What d'you make of that?" he asked.

"What is it? Is it money? Where did you find it?"

"I excavated it."

"You didn't! Where?"

"In our garden. By the bonfire heap. I was just digging a bit, to see if there might be anything – you never know – and I dug this up."

"It must be ancient!" said Milly-Molly-Mandy. "Have you shown it to anybody?"

"Not yet." Billy Blunt rubbed it carefully with his handkerchief. "Mother's busy, and Dad's got customers."

"Let's show it to Mr Rudge!" said Milly-Molly-Mandy. "He knows about iron and such things; he'll know if it's valuable."

So they went along to the forge, where the

blacksmith was blowing up his fire.

Milly-Molly-Mandy peeped in the doorway.

"Mr Rudge! Billy Blunt's excavated some-thing!" she told him. "And we want to know if you think it's very valuable!"

The blacksmith looked round with a twinkle in his eye. He held out one great grimy hand, working the bellows with the other, and Billy Blunt put the precious coin into it.

Mr Rudge examined it one side, then the other. Then he rubbed it on his big leather apron and looked again.

"Hmmm," he said solemnly. "Georgian, I'd say. Yes. Undoubtedly."

"Is that very ancient?" asked Milly-Molly-Mandy.

"What's it worth?" asked Billy Blunt.

"If you're asking me, don't you take a ha'penny less than a penny for it. But mind you," he added, "if it's treasure-trove it may belong to the Crown."

He gave the coin back and turned again to his fire. Billy Blunt and Milly-Molly-Mandy came out into the sunshine, looking to see what all that rubbing had done.

"Looks like there's a head –" said Billy Blunt; "can't see any date."

"What's treasure-trove mean?" asked Milly-Molly-Mandy.

"Dunno. P'raps if you dig up treasure you aren't supposed to keep it."

Then Milly-Molly-Mandy had an idea.

"If you dug this out of your garden maybe there's some more there! Can't you go excavating again? I'll help."

So they went back to the Blunts's garden, beside the corn-shop, and Billy Blunt led the way round the rhubarb-bed to the end by the rubbish-heap and the bonfire.

He picked up a trowel and handed Milly-Molly-Mandy a rusty knife to dig with, and they began jabbing about in the earth and weeds. But there didn't seem to be anything else but stones. (Plenty of them.)

Presently Milly-Molly-Mandy said:

"It's awfully hard under here – feels like rock."

"Where?" said Billy Blunt. He came over and used his trowel. "Looks like cement."

"Perhaps it's buried treasure cemented in!" said Milly-Molly-Mandy.

"Fetch a spade out of the shed there," ordered Billy Blunt. "Hurry!"

So Milly-Molly-Mandy ran and fetched him a spade, and she took over the trowel. And they could see there was something, underneath the earth and weeds!

"It's got an iron lid!" panted Milly-Molly-Mandy.

"It's an iron chest, cemented down!" puffed Billy Blunt.

They got the top scraped clear. It was square and rusty, with a kind of loop to lift it by.

"This is buried treasure all right!"

Billy Blunt was red with excitement.

Milly-Molly-Mandy wanted to jump and shout, but she was too busy.

The lid was awfully heavy. They tried to lever it up, but they couldn't.

"You'll have to tell your father and mother, won't you?" said Milly-Molly-Mandy, at last.

Billy Blunt dropped the spade and dashed indoors. And presently Mr Blunt came out, in his apron, and walked over to their hole.

He took one look.

"*That?*" he said. "Whatever will you be up to next? That's only the cover of the drain!" When he could stop laughing he added, "Just as well you unearthed it, though – there might have been trouble if the authorities knew it had got covered over. Don't know how it happened."

"But look, Dad. I found this –" Billy Blunt showed his piece of money. "We thought there might be some more. It's quite ancient, isn't it? The blacksmith said Georgian."

Mr Blunt scraped with his pocket knife a moment. Then he fished a few coins from his trousers' pocket, picked out a penny and handed it over with the other. "There's your same Georgian coin," he chuckled, "King George V – only a bit cleaner. Yours looks as if it's been on the bonfire!"

Well! It was all very disappointing. But anyhow, those two pennies bought two fine peppermint humbugs from Miss Muggins's shop. And, sucking away together, Billy Blunt and Milly-Molly-Mandy both agreed it had really been quite fun while it lasted.

But they hoped the excavators up on Hooker's Hill were having better luck!

MILLY-MOLLY-MANDY
GOES SLEDGING

ONCE UPON A TIME, one cold grey wintry day, Milly-Molly-Mandy and the others were coming home from school.

It was such a cold wintry day that everybody turned up their coat-collars and put their hands in their pockets, and such a grey wintry day that it seemed almost dark already, though it was only four o'clock.

"Oooh! isn't it a cold grey wintry day!" said Milly-Molly-Mandy.

"Perhaps it's going to snow," said little-friend-Susan.

"Hope it does," said Billy Blunt. "I'm going to make a sledge."

Whereupon Milly-Molly-Mandy and little-friend-Susan said both together: "Ooh! will you give us a ride on it?"

"Haven't made it yet," said Billy Blunt. "But I've got an old wooden box I can make it of."

Then he said goodbye and went in at the side gate by the corn-shop where he lived. And Milly-Molly-Mandy and little-friend-Susan ran together along the road to the Moggs's cottage, where little-friend-Susan lived. And then Milly-Molly-Mandy went on alone to the nice white cottage with the thatched roof, where Toby the dog came capering out to welcome her home.

It felt so nice and warm in the kitchen, and it smelled so nice and warm too, that Milly-Molly-Mandy was quite glad to be in.

"Here she comes!" said Grandma, putting the well-filled toast-rack on the table.

"There you are!" said Aunty, breaking open hot scones and buttering them on a plate.

"Just in time, Milly-Molly-Mandy!" said Mother, pouring boiling water into the teapot. "Call the men-folk in to tea, but don't keep the door open long."

So Milly-Molly-Mandy called, and Father and Grandpa and Uncle soon came in, rubbing their hands, very pleased to get back into the warm again.

"Ah! Nicer indoors than out," said Grandpa.

"There's snow in the air," said Uncle.

"Shouldn't wonder if we had a fall before morning," said Father.

"Billy Blunt's going to make a sledge, and he *might* let Susan and me have a ride, if it snows," said Milly-Molly-Mandy. And she wished very much that it would.

That set Father and Uncle talking during tea of the fun they used to have in their young days sledging down Crocker's Hill.

Milly-Molly-Mandy did wish it would snow soon.

The next day was Saturday, and there was no school, which always made it feel different when you woke up in the morning. But all the same Milly-Molly-Mandy thought something about her little bedroom looked different somehow, when she opened her eyes.

"Milly-Molly-Mandy!" called Mother up the stairs, as she did every morning.

"Yoo-oo!" called Milly-Molly-Mandy, to show she was awake.

"Have you looked out of your window yet?" called Mother.

"No, Mother," called Milly-Molly-Mandy, sitting up in bed. "Why?"

"You look," said Mother. "And hurry up with your dressing." And she went downstairs to the kitchen to get the breakfast.

So Milly-Molly-Mandy jumped out of bed and looked.

"Oh!" she said, staring. "Oh-h!"

For everything outside her little low window was white as white could be, except the sky, which was dark, dirty grey and criss-crossed all over with snowflakes flying down.

"Oh-h-h!" said Milly-Molly-Mandy again.

And then she set to work washing and dressing in a great hurry (and wasn't it cold!) and she rushed downstairs.

She wanted to go out and play at once, almost before she had done breakfast, but Mother said there was plenty of time to clear up all her porridge, for she mustn't go out until the snow stopped falling.

Milly-Molly-Mandy hoped it would be quick and stop. She wanted to see little-friend-Susan, and to find out if Billy Blunt had begun making his sledge.

But Father said, the deeper the snow the better for sledging. So then Milly-Molly-Mandy didn't know whether she most wished it to snow or to stop snowing!

"Well," said Mother, "it looks as if it means to go on snowing for some while yet, so I should wish for that if I were you! Suppose you be Jemima-Jane and help me to make the cakes this morning, as you can't go out."

So Milly-Molly-Mandy tied on an apron and became Jemima-Jane. And she washed up the breakfast things and put them away; and fetched whatever Mother wanted for

cake-making from the larder and the cup-
board, and picked over the sultanas (which
was a nice job, as Jemima-Jane was allowed
to eat as many sultanas as she had fingers on
both hands, but not one more), and she beat
the eggs in a basin, and stirred the cake-mix-
ture in the bowl. And after Mother had filled
the cake tins Jemima-Jane was allowed to put
the scrapings into her own little patty-pan and
bake it for her own self in the oven (and that
sort of cake always tastes nicer than any other
sort, only there's never enough of it!)

Well, it snowed and it snowed all day. Milly-
Molly-Mandy kept running to the windows to

look, but it didn't stop once. When Father and Grandpa and Uncle had to go out (to see after the cows and the pony and the chickens) they came back looking like snowmen.

"Is it good for sledging yet, Father?" asked Milly-Molly-Mandy.

"Getting better every minute, Milly-Molly-Mandy, that's certain," answered Father, stamping snow off his boots on the door-mat.

"I wonder what Susan thinks of it, and if Billy has nearly made his sledge yet," said Milly-Molly-Mandy.

But it didn't stop snowing before dark, so she couldn't find out that day.

The next day, Sunday, the snow had stopped falling, and it looked beautiful, spread out all over everything. Father and Mother and Grandpa and Uncle and Aunty and Milly-Molly-Mandy put on their Wellington boots, or goloshes (Milly-Molly-Mandy had boots), and walked to Church. (Grandma didn't like walking in the snow, so she stayed at home to look after the fire and put the potatoes on.)

Billy Blunt was there with his father and mother, so afterwards in the lane Milly-Molly-

Mandy asked him, "Have you made your sledge yet?"

And Billy Blunt said, "'Tisn't finished. Dad's going to help me with it this afternoon. I'll be trying it out before school to-morrow, probably."

Milly-Molly-Mandy was sorry it wasn't done yet. But anyhow she and little-friend-Susan had a grand time all that afternoon, making a snowman in the Moggs's front garden.

On Monday Milly-Molly-Mandy was in a great hurry to finish her breakfast and be off very early to school.

She didn't have long to wait for little-friend-Susan either, and together they trudged along through the snow. It was quite hard going, for sometimes it was almost over the tops of their boots. (But they didn't always keep to the road!)

When they came to the village there, just outside the corn-shop, was Billy Blunt's new sledge. And while they were looking at it Billy Blunt came out at the side gate.

"Hullo," he said. "Thought you weren't coming."

"Hullo, Billy. Isn't that a beauty! Have you been on it yet? Can we have a ride?"

"You'll have to hurry, then," said Billy Blunt, picking up the string. "I've been up on the hill by Crocker's Farm, past the crossroads."

"I know," said Milly-Molly-Mandy, "near where that little girl Bunchy and her grand-mother live. Can we go there now?"

"Hurry up, then," said Billy Blunt.

So they all hurried up, through the village, past the crossroads and the school, along the road to Crocker's Hill, shuffling through the snow, dragging the sledge behind them.

"Isn't it deep here!" panted Milly-Molly-Mandy. "This is the way Bunchy comes to school every day. I wonder how she'll manage today. She isn't very big."

"We've come uphill a long way," panted little-friend-Susan. "Can't we sit on the sledge and go down now?"

"Oh, let's get to the top of the hill first," panted Milly-Molly-Mandy.

"There's a steep bit there. You get a good run," said Billy Blunt. "I've done it six times. I went up before breakfast."

"I wish I'd come too!" said Milly-Molly-Mandy.

"Sledge only holds one," said Billy Blunt.

"Oh!" said Milly-Molly-Mandy.

"Oh!" said little-friend-Susan.

They hadn't thought of that.

"Which of us has first go?" said little-friend-Susan.

"Don't suppose there'll be time for more than one of you, anyhow," said Billy Blunt. "We've got to get back."

"You have first go," said Milly-Molly-Mandy to little-friend-Susan.

"No, you have first go," said little-friend-Susan to Milly-Molly-Mandy.

"Better hurry," said Billy Blunt. "You'll be late for school."

They struggled on up the last steep bit of the hill.

And there were the little girl Bunchy and her grandmother, hand-in-hand, struggling up it through the snow from the other side. The little cottage where they lived could be seen down below, with their two sets of footprints leading up from it.

"Hullo, Bunchy," said Milly-Molly-Mandy.

"Oh! Hullo, Milly-Molly-Mandy," said Bunchy.

And Bunchy and her grandmother both looked very pleased to see them all. Grandmother had just been thinking she would have to take Bunchy all the way to school today.

But Milly-Molly-Mandy said, "I'll take care of her." And she took hold of Bunchy's little cold hand with her warm one (it was very warm indeed with pulling the sledge up the

hill). "You go down in the sledge, Susan, and I'll look after Bunchy."

"No," said little-friend-Susan. "You wanted it just as much."

"Sit *her* on it," said Billy Blunt, pointing to Bunchy. "We can run her to school in no time. Come on."

So Bunchy had the ride, with Billy Blunt to guide the sledge and Milly-Molly-Mandy and little-friend-Susan to keep her safe on it. And Grandmother stood and watched them all go shouting down the steep bit. And then, as Bunchy was quite light and the road was a bit downhill most of the way, they pulled her along easily, right up to the school gate, in good time for school.

And Bunchy *did* enjoy her ride. She thought it was the excitingest thing that had ever happened!

And then after afternoon school (Bunchy had her dinner at school because it was too far for her to go home for it) Billy Blunt told her to get on his sledge again. And he and Milly-Molly-Mandy and little-friend-Susan pulled her all the way home (except up the steepest bit). And

Grandmother was so grateful to them that she gave them each a warm currant bun.

And then Milly-Molly-Mandy and little-friend-Susan took turns riding down the hill on Billy Blunt's sledge. It went like the wind, so that you had to shriek like anything, and your cap blew off, and you felt you could go on for ever! And then, *Whoosh!* you landed sprawling in the snow just where the road turned near the bottom.

Milly-Molly-Mandy and little-friend-Susan each got tipped out there. But when Billy Blunt had gone back to the top of the hill with the sledge for his turn he came sailing down and rounded the bend like a bird, and went on and on and was almost at the crossroads when the others caught him up. (But then, he'd had plenty of practice, and nobody had seen him spill out at his first try!)

It seemed a long walk home to the nice white cottage with the thatched roof after all that, and Milly-Molly-Mandy was quite late for tea. But Father and Mother and Grandpa and Grandma and Uncle and Aunty weren't a bit cross, because they guessed what she had been up to, and of course, you can't go sledging every day!

In fact, it rained that very night, and next day the snow was nearly gone. So wasn't it a good thing that Billy Blunt had got his sledge made in time?